Dear DADDY I LOVE YOU

Published by Hinkler Books Pty Ltd
45–55 Fairchild Street
Heatherton Victoria 3202 Australia
www.hinkler.com.au

hinkler

© Hinkler Books Pty Ltd 2014

Author: Catherine Allison
Illustrator: Shelagh McNicholas

ISBN: 978 1 7436 3284 0

Printed and bound in China

Dear DADDY I LOVE YOU

Catherine Allison • Shelagh McNicholas

hinkler

Dear Daddy.
I love you very much! Let me tell you when...

At help-me-do-them-up time.

At 'walkies!'-by-the-sea time.

At come-back-dog! time.

And all-clean-now time.

At watch-me-race time.

And proud-of-me-for-doing-my-best time.

At yummy-hot-dog time.

And have-some-of-mine time.

At quiet-snuggle time.

At show-me-how time.

And my turn now time.

At itchy-scratchy-haircut time.

And can-I-come-again? time.

At best-kick-at-goal time.

And oops-too-hard! time.

At rainy-day-fun time.

At can't-stay-awake time.

And good-night-sleep-tight time.

So you see. I love you all the time.

You're the best daddy in the world!

Here are some ways you can decorate this card
to make a special message for Daddy.

Draw a picture of Daddy.

Take a photo of you and
Daddy and paste it to the card.

Make a handprint with paint.